THE LIBRARY OF FUTURE WEAPONRY™

UNDERWATER WARFARE OF THE FUTURE

Krista West

The Rosen Publishing Group, Inc., New York

Published in 2006 by The Rosen Publishing Group, Inc.
29 East 21st Street, New York, NY 10010

Copyright © 2006 by The Rosen Publishing Group, Inc.

First Edition

Library of Congress Cataloging-in-Publication Data

West, Krista.
Underwater warfare of the future/Krista West.
    p. cm.—(The library of future weaponry)
ISBN 1-4042-0522-5 (library binding)
1. Submarine warfare—Juvenile literature. 2. Submarines (Ships)—Juvenile literature. I. Title. II. Series.
V210.W437 2005
359.9'3—dc22
                                                                                2005012467

Manufactured in the United States of America

On the cover: A conceptual drawing of a future Virginia-class attack submarine.

CONTENTS

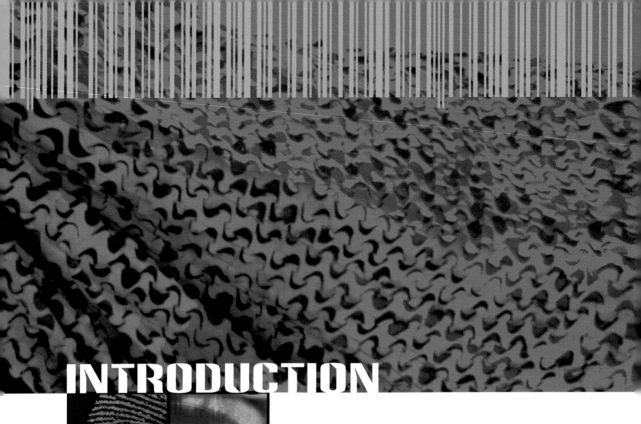

INTRODUCTION

Ping. Ping. Ping. A blinking light charts your course on a dimly lit black screen. Ping. Ping. Ping. You cannot see the sky. You cannot see the ground. You are surrounded by dark, cold ocean water. The technology of the pinging screen is the only way to know your location on the planet. You are in a submarine.

Submarines are the quarterbacks in the game of underwater warfare—you can't really play without them. Submarines carry, transport, and deploy specialized weapons for underwater wars. And they do it quieter, sneakier, and better than any other vessel.

Because of the unique characteristics of submarines, many submarine missions that are conducted by the United States Navy are top secret. We know that the navy operates about seventy submarines today. In the future, the military hopes to have even more submarines in operation. The fleet is growing partly because no other vessel can substitute for the submarine, and partly because they are pretty affordable for the navy to run.

Currently, submarines make up 30 percent of the navy's fleet, but use only 9 percent of its people and 12 percent of its budget. Basically, it doesn't take much money or manpower to run lots of submarines. That's important, because submarines have a lot of work to do.

Modern submarines are used for five main purposes. The first role of a submarine is to collect information in secret. A submarine can sit in one place for a long time and monitor what's happening in the air, sea, or on nearby land and report back to commanders. The second role is to locate underwater bombs called mines and warn others of the mine locations, saving lives and vessels. The third role of a submarine is to safely transport and pick up soldiers on secret missions. The fourth role is to patrol and protect the oceans, monitoring shipping lanes and countering enemy ships and subs. Lastly, submarines can be used to launch missiles at ground targets.

To carry out these and other jobs, submarines use a combination of offensive and defensive weapons systems that are as unique and specialized as the submarine itself. This book will explore the future of some of these underwater weapons systems: sonar, torpedoes, robots, specially trained marine mammals, and nonlethal weapons.

Scientists and engineers employed by the navy are constantly working to improve old weapons systems and develop new ones. As a result, the underwater weapons discussed in this book are in different stages of development—some are small improvements on existing weapons systems, others are simply ideas for new weapons that may or may not become reality in the future.

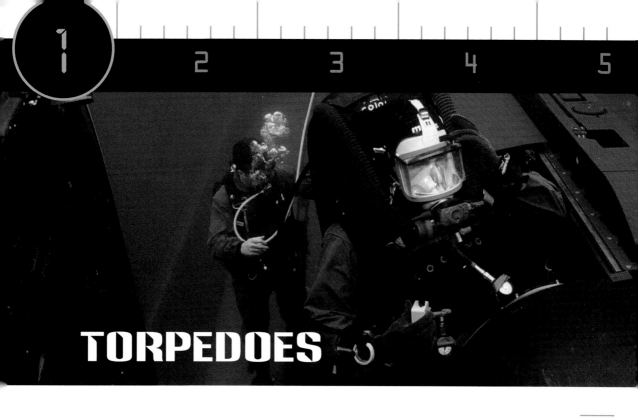

TORPEDOES

They are silent. They are fast. And they are able to sink ships and submarines in a single shot. They are torpedoes— one of the navy's deadliest and most commonly used underwater weapons.

Torpedoes have been in use for more than a hundred years. In the past twenty years, the U.S. Navy has tweaked and steadily improved these reliable weapons. Only in the past couple years has a completely new type of torpedo been invented. If all goes as planned, tomorrow's torpedo will be around for another hundred years.

Torpedoes are basically moving bombs with brains. They often look like oversized bullets with propellers on one end, capable of propelling themselves and exploding on or near a target.

Sailors handle an MK46 torpedo aboard the USS *Mustin*. An MK46 is about 8 feet (2.5 meters) long and travels underwater at more than 30 miles per hour (48 kilometers per hour). In the future, the navy plans to replace the MK46 with the MK50, a slightly larger and faster torpedo.

THE VERSATILE TORPEDO

One thing that makes torpedoes so valuable in underwater warfare is that they work in many different situations. They can be launched from ships, submarines, and airplanes. They go after targets in deep or shallow water. They also come in many different sizes and weights. Not many other weapons are as versatile as the torpedo.

THE U.S. NAVY'S SUBMARINE FLEET

The U.S. Navy currently operates two types of submarines: attack submarines and ballistic missile submarines. Both are nuclear powered, which means the engines are fueled by an element called uranium that provides almost unlimited high-speed power.

You can identify a submarine's type from its name. Attack submarines always have "SSN" in their names. "SS" is the designation for a submarine and "N" is short for "nuclear powered." Ballistic missile submarines always include "SSBN" in the name—which identifies the vessel as a nuclear-powered submarine carrying a ballistic ("B") missile. Each type of submarine has its own specialty during wartime.

Attack submarines are designed to seek and destroy enemy submarines and surface ships in close range. They are fast and carry dozens of torpedoes. They can also carry Tomahawk cruise missiles, which can be launched at land targets. The U.S. Navy currently uses three different classes, or models, of attack submarines: the Virginia class, the Seawolf class, and the Los Angeles class. Of these, the Virginia-class submarines are the newest vessels, with some still under construction for future use.

Ballistic missile submarines carry long-range nuclear missiles capable of attacking a target thousands of miles away. Each submarine is designed to carry twenty-four of these missiles plus a handful of short-range torpedoes. There is only one class of ballistic missile submarines in operation today—the Ohio class.

A technician inspects a torpedo tube inside the Los Angeles–class attack submarine USS *Portsmouth*. The tube is designed to launch an MK48 ADCAP torpedo. This type of torpedo is carried by every attack submarine in the navy's force.

SEEK AND DESTROY

Today's torpedoes are equipped with technologies that act as the weapons' eyes and flippers. A torpedo "sees" with a homing system and "swims" using battery- or fuel-powered propellers. These two systems work together, with the help of computers, to make the torpedo a persistent and smart weapon.

If a torpedo misses its target on the first try, for example, it will use its homing system to find the target again. The homing system sends out little pings of sound that travel through the water. If there is nothing in front of the ping, the sound keeps traveling away from the torpedo. But if there's something in the water, the ping bounces off the object and travels back to let the torpedo know something is there.

Once the homing device receives a sound signal that matches the description of its target, computers help locate the object in the water. The torpedo is redirected toward the object for another attack. If the torpedo misses the target, it can be programmed to attack again and again on its own until the target is destroyed.

MK48 ADCAP

One torpedo carried by all U.S. Navy attack submarines today is called the MK48 advanced capability heavyweight (ADCAP). The MK48 ADCAP is 19 feet long (5.8 m), 20 inches wide (51 centimeters), weighs almost 4,000 pounds (1,814 kilograms), and can travel more than 30 miles per hour underwater (48 km per hour).

The MK48 ADCAP is designed to go after deep-diving submarines and quick-moving ships on the surface. Once launched from a submarine, a little wire antenna spins out from the torpedo allowing the submarine and the torpedo to communicate. The onboard operator can then use the submarine's sophisticated computer systems to help guide the torpedo to its target, avoiding decoys and jamming devices that might otherwise throw the torpedo off course. When the torpedo is on the right track, the communicating wire is dropped and the torpedo operates on its own.

The navy has more than 1,000 MK48 ADCAP torpedoes in its stock (each costs about $3 million to build), and is constantly

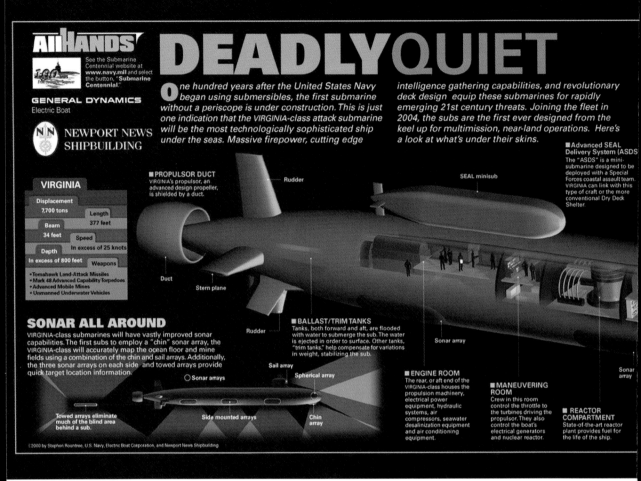

AllHANDS

See the Submarine Centennial website at **www.navy.mil** and select the button, "Submarine Centennial."

GENERAL DYNAMICS
Electric Boat

NEWPORT NEWS SHIPBUILDING

DEADLYQUIET

One hundred years after the United States Navy began using submersibles, the first submarine without a periscope is under construction. This is just one indication that the VIRGINIA-class attack submarine will be the most technologically sophisticated ship under the seas. Massive firepower, cutting edge intelligence gathering capabilities, and revolutionary deck design equip these submarines for rapidly emerging 21st century threats. Joining the fleet in 2004, the subs are the first ever designed from the keel up for multimission, near-land operations. Here's a look at what's under their skins.

■ Advanced SEAL Delivery System (ASDS) The "ASDS" is a mini-submarine designed to be deployed with a Special Forces coastal assault team. VIRGINIA can link with this type of craft or the more conventional Dry Deck Shelter.

VIRGINIA

Displacement	
7,700 tons	
	Length
Beam	377 feet
34 feet	Speed
Depth	In excess of 25 knots
In excess of 800 feet	Weapons

• Tomahawk Land-Attack Missiles
• Mark 48 Advanced Capability Torpedoes
• Advanced Mobile Mines
• Unmanned Underwater Vehicles

■ PROPULSOR DUCT VIRGINIA's propulsor, an advanced design propeller, is shielded by a duct.

Rudder

SEAL minisub

Duct

Stern plane

SONAR ALL AROUND

VIRGINIA-class submarines will have vastly improved sonar capabilities. The first subs to employ a "chin" sonar array, the VIRGINIA-class will accurately map the ocean floor and mine fields using a combination of the chin and sail arrays. Additionally, the three sonar arrays on each side and towed arrays provide quick target location information.

■ BALLAST/TRIM TANKS Tanks, both forward and aft, are flooded with water to submerge the sub. The water is ejected in order to surface. Other tanks, "trim tanks," help compensate for variations in weight, stabilizing the sub.

Rudder

Sonar array

Sail array

○ Sonar arrays

Spherical array

Sonar array

Towed arrays eliminate much of the blind area behind a sub.

Side mounted arrays

Chin array

■ ENGINE ROOM The rear, or aft end of the VIRGINIA-class houses the propulsion machinery, electrical power equipment, hydraulic systems, air compressors, seawater desalinization equipment and air conditioning equipment.

■ MANEUVERING ROOM Crew in this room control the throttle to the turbines driving the propulsor. They also control the boat's electrical generators and nuclear reactor.

■ REACTOR COMPARTMENT State-of-the-art reactor plant provides fuel for the life of the ship.

©2000 by Stephen Rountree, U.S. Navy, Electric Boat Corporation, and Newport News Shipbuilding

Above is an illustration of the USS *Virginia*, the lead sub of the Virginia class of attack submarines. The *Virginia* officially joined the navy's fleet on October 23, 2004. Its amazing ability to avoid detection by the enemy will make it the premiere underwater weapon of the twenty-first century.

working to improve its technology. It calls the MK48 ADCAP the "workhorse of the fleet," meaning it is one of the most commonly used and most reliable weapons.

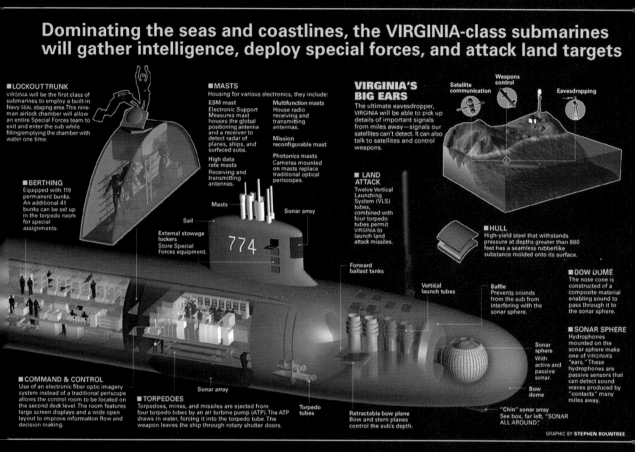

Dominating the seas and coastlines, the VIRGINIA-class submarines will gather intelligence, deploy special forces, and attack land targets

■ LOCKOUT TRUNK
VIRGINIA will be the first class of submarines to employ a built-in Navy SEAL staging area. This nine-man airlock chamber will allow an entire Special Forces team to exit and enter the sub while filling/emptying the chamber with water one time.

■ BERTHING
Equipped with 119 permanent bunks. An additional 41 bunks can be set up in the torpedo room for special assignments.

■ MASTS
Housing for various electronics, they include:
ESM mast
Electronic Support Measures mast houses the global positioning antenna and a receiver to detect radar of planes, ships, and surfaced subs.

Multifunction masts
House radio receiving and transmitting antennas.

Mission reconfigurable mast

High data rate masts
Receiving and transmitting antennas.

Photonics masts
Cameras mounted on masts replace traditional optical periscopes.

VIRGINIA'S BIG EARS
The ultimate eavesdropper, VIRGINIA will be able to pick up details of important signals from miles away—signals our satellites can't detect. It can also talk to satellites and control weapons.

■ LAND ATTACK
Twelve Vertical Launching System (VLS) tubes, combined with four torpedo tubes permit VIRGINIA to launch land attack missiles.

Satellite communication

Weapons control

Eavesdropping

■ HULL
High-yield steel that withstands pressure at depths greater than 800 feet has a seamless rubberlike substance molded onto its surface.

■ BOW DOME
The nose cone is constructed of a composite material enabling sound to pass through it to the sonar sphere.

■ SONAR SPHERE
Hydrophones mounted on the sonar sphere make one of VIRGINIA's "ears." These hydrophones are passive sensors that can detect sound waves produced by "contacts" many miles away.

Sail
External stowage lockers
Store Special Forces equipment.

Masts
774
Sonar array
Forward ballast tanks

Vertical launch tubes

Baffle
Prevents sounds from the sub from interfering with the sonar sphere.

Sonar sphere
With active and passive sonar.

Bow dome

"Chin" sonar array
See box, far left, "SONAR ALL AROUND."

■ COMMAND & CONTROL
Use of an electronic fiber optic imagery system instead of a traditional periscope allows the control room to be located on the second deck level. The room features large screen displays and a wide open layout to improve information flow and decision making.

Sonar array

■ TORPEDOES
Torpedoes, mines, and missiles are ejected from four torpedo tubes by an air turbine pump (ATP). The ATP draws in water, forcing it into the torpedo tube. The weapon leaves the ship through rotary shutter doors.

Torpedo tubes

Retractable bow plane
Bow and stern planes control the sub's depth.

GRAPHIC BY **STEPHEN ROUNTREE**

TOMORROW'S TORPEDOES

In the future, torpedoes will have all the abilities of the MK48 ADCAP, but will be even better. Tomorrow's torpedoes will be stealthier, faster, bigger, and smarter.

Stealthier

To be stealthy means to be ultraquiet and to move without being detected. Noises given off by today's torpedoes can sometimes let

TRY TORPEDOES FOR YOURSELF

Looking to get a ride on a submarine? While the navy doesn't do many submarine tours, Val Schmidt, a submarine engineer at the Lamont-Doherty Earth Observatory at Columbia University in New York City, says a video game may be the next best thing. Schmidt has worked on many submarines and says the *SubCommand* video game simulates the real thing better than anything he's ever seen.

Don't be fooled. Like working on a real submarine, this game is not easy. Your job is to monitor multiple control panels to see who's in your area and who can see you. Once you have assembled the pieces of the puzzle that make up your surroundings, you can decide whether to launch a torpedo.

the enemy know the torpedo is coming. This gives the enemy time to get out of the way, send a decoy to confuse the torpedo, or fire back. The pinging and propeller noises made by the MK48, for example, often give the torpedo's location away to the enemy.

Future torpedoes will have nonpinging, or passive, homing systems that let the torpedo see without being seen. Instead of using sound to detect an object underwater, the torpedo will use radiation (heat) that cannot be heard or easily detected by the enemy.

To quiet the sounds of the propellers, the motor and the propellers themselves will be changed somewhat. The MK48 ADCAP has a separate, large, internal motor that is connected to the propellers on the end. On future torpedoes, the motor and the propellers will be the same piece of equipment, making the motor smaller and quieter. Plus, by changing the distance and angle between the individual propeller blades, some sound can be reduced. Combining these changes not only makes the propellers stealthier, it lets the torpedo leave less of a path in the water.

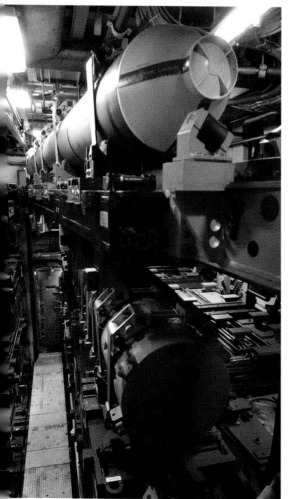

Faster

The faster a torpedo moves, the faster it can hit a target before the enemy has time to react. The navy says future torpedoes will move five times faster than the MK48 by using a process called supercavitation.

Above is a view of the cramped quarters in the torpedo room of the USS *Jimmy Carter*. The *Jimmy Carter* joined the U.S. Navy force in February 2005. The sub is the third and final member of the Seawolf class.

Supercavitation means that a small pocket of water in front of a torpedo is vaporized. This creates a space filled with air directly in front of the torpedo so that the torpedo can "fly" forward. By continually vaporizing the water in its path, a torpedo flies through a stream of air under the water.

Since air is much lighter than water, objects can move through air with less effort or work. Because there is less work to do, the torpedo is able to fly much faster than it could ever swim, allowing it to surprise enemies more effectively. As of 2004, only Russia is known to have torpedoes with supercavitation technology. The U.S. Navy has begun testing supercavitation torpedoes and hopes to have them on submarines in the future.

Bigger

For a torpedo to be a good weapon it has to carry some punch. Today's torpedoes come in two sizes. Lightweight torpedoes, the kind dropped from airplanes and helicopters, carry about 100 pounds (45 kg) of explosives. Heavyweight torpedoes, the kind launched from ships and submarines, carry about 1,000 pounds (454 kg) of explosives.

Torpedoes of the future will carry more explosive power but be smaller and lighter. The military is secretive about exactly what kinds and how many explosives the torpedoes of tomorrow will carry. One thing that is known, according to the navy's Web site, is that tomorrow's torpedoes will have "more bang for the buck."

Smarter

Antitorpedoes are the only truly new type of torpedo invented in the past twenty years. The job of an antitorpedo is to destroy incoming enemy torpedoes. Compared to regular torpedoes, antitorpedoes are small—about 9 feet (2.7 m) long and only 7 inches (17.8 cm) in diameter.

Already in development by the U.S. military, antitorpedo testers have been fired from underwater guns. By vaporizing the water in their paths using supercavitation technology, they have broken the speed of sound in water, about 3,300 miles per hour (5,311 km/h).

Such weapons could be fired from the water or the air at enemy torpedoes and underwater mines, creating a completely new type of underwater weapon. Antitorpedoes will play a big role in underwater wars of the future.

SONAR

In combat situations, sometimes being able to see the enemy clearly is a weapon in itself. Night vision goggles help soldiers see at night, radar lets pilots see in the sky, and sonar helps submarines see underwater.

In the past, sonar systems were a few bulky gadgets towed behind a submarine. Today, sonar systems include hundreds of miniature sensors with high-speed digital parts. As science continues to improve, submarine sonar will continue to improve how well and how far it can see. This improved sonar will help the navy learn more about the enemy during warfare.

Submarines use two basic types of sonar: active and passive. An active sonar system generates a wave of sound that spreads outward until it bumps into something and bounces back. The sound wave that comes back can provide information about what it hit in the water—a whale, the ground, or

The USS *Virginia* is seen under construction in this photo taken on August 5, 2003. The green circles indicate the location of components of the submarine's sonar system known as arrays. An array is a collection of microphones that detects underwater sounds. The *Virginia* also has an additional array in the front, or chin, of the submarine that cannot be seen in this photograph.

another vessel. Passive sonar only receives incoming sound waves produced by other objects, such as torpedoes or submarines, in the water.

TODAY'S SONAR

Modern navy submarines have many types of sonar on board that are used for different purposes. Some systems are mounted inside the hull of the vessel, and some are towed in lines behind submarines.

The wide aperture array (WAA) is a modern sonar system mounted inside the hulls of attack submarines. It is a passive-type

THE FUTURE OF U.S. SUBMARINES

For many decades in the mid- to late-twentieth century, the United States and the Soviet Union were not friendly. This unfriendly tension became known worldwide as the Cold War. During this period, the navy's submarine fleet was beefed up in case the two countries really started fighting. The United States had plans to build nearly 100 new submarines to defend against the Soviet Union.

Then in 1991, the Soviet Union collapsed and the Cold War ended without any fighting. Suddenly, the United States didn't need to build so many submarines. Construction plans changed, and some working submarines were taken out of service. For the submarine fleet, this was a big cut in money and support. The navy had to decide what the future submarine fleet might look like.

The Virginia-class attack submarine USS *Texas*, seen under construction in April 2005, is expected to be ready for service by May 2006.

After lots of thought and discussion by experts, the navy decided the United States still needs a good submarine fleet. The fleet would be used to defend against enemy countries, and also to support military forces on the ground. Today, the navy has fifty-five attack submarines and eighteen ballistic missile submarines.

The next generation of navy submarines will be mostly Virginia-class attack submarines. These submarines work well in shallow waters and are cheap to build. Designed entirely on computers, the navy says Virginia-class submarines are smaller and quieter than any other type of submarine.

The first Virginia-class submarine became part of the navy fleet in October 2004. It is manned by a crew of 134 sailors. Its weapons include Tomahawk cruise missiles and MK48 ADCAP torpedoes. Additional Virginia-class submarines will be constructed and gradually added to the fleet over the next fifteen years.

system. The WAA consists of six ordered groups, or arrays, of 450 underwater microphones. These microphones, known as hydrophones, can detect sounds made by enemy targets that are very far away. This allows the sub to detect the enemy before being seen itself. The submarine can then fire a weapon at the enemy before the enemy has a chance to react.

To find targets that don't make very much noise or targets in shallow waters, active towed sonar arrays work well. These strings of hydrophones can be just a couple feet long or span half a football field. They are dragged behind a submarine as it moves through the water. They can be turned on when needed to find particularly sneaky targets. As submarines have become quieter and stealthier, active sonar arrays have become more valuable.

TOMORROW'S SONAR

Future sonar systems will include technically improved versions of what we have today, plus some new inventions.

3-D Sonar

The trick to improving today's sonar systems is finding a way to make them work better in the three-dimensional world. If you imagine being underwater, you can look in front and behind you (one dimension), from side-to-side (two dimensions), and up and down (three dimensions).

In most modern sonar systems, the hydrophones are arranged in only one or two dimensions. Imagine standing in the middle of a long line of hydrophones (like the kind you would find in a towed array). You could look from one end of the line to the other because it is a one-dimensional setup.

These types of systems work best in the number of dimensions for which they are designed. For example, two-dimensional systems work well in two dimensions, but not so well in three. In the future, finding ways to arrange hydrophones to make them work better in three dimensions will allow submarines to collect better information.

Autopilot Submarines

Surface ships can use sonar to steer the ship without a pilot, cutting down on needed manpower in warfare situations. However, putting a submarine on sonar autopilot is not yet possible. The submarine's computers cannot process the information returned by a sonar system fast enough to use it to steer a course. Computers onboard submarines will have to process information faster in order to make an autopilot system work in the future.

Mobile Arrays

Some of today's towed arrays can be disconnected from the submarine and allowed to move around freely in the water. This is known as a mobile array. In the future, mobile arrays could be lighter to make them easier to maneuver once disconnected from the submarine. Plus, they could operate automatically so that fewer people would be needed in warfare situations. If mobile arrays operated reliably far away from a submarine, it would give the military a way to gather information without risk of being caught in a dangerous situation.

Beam Sonar

Imagine being able to point sonar at the bottom of the seafloor like a flashlight. This is what beam sonar does. It highlights a circular area of seafloor and returns information about it. To do this right requires a lot of hydrophones, energy, and computer memory. It is often used today by scientists to map the seafloor.

Crewmen hoist a Klein 5000 side scan sonar. The Klein 5000 uses multiple beams to scan the ocean floor for man-made objects such as mines. The main unit of the system is called a towfish. It trails behind the ship and sends back data through an attached cable. The multiple beams of the Klein 5000 allow it to scan larger areas of the seafloor than a single-beam sonar system can.

In a warfare situation, a military submarine might use beam sonar as a defensive weapon. If a submarine can find a large underwater mountain or valley, it might be able to hide from an enemy by resting on the ocean floor. When enemy sonar scans the mountain, the hidden submarine might look like part of the mountain. The better we can see the seafloor, the more hiding places we can find in the future.

TOMORROW'S SONAR CHALLENGE

How sound travels underwater depends heavily on the underwater environment—whether it is shallow or deep, with a smooth or bumpy seafloor. Since these things affect sound, they

LAYERS OF OCEAN

The ocean is made up of layers of water that vary in temperature and pressure. Sound waves travel very differently through the different layers of water, affecting how sonar works.

In a well-known layer called the SOFAR (sound fixing and ranging) channel, temperatures and pressures combine to make sound travel particularly fast. Think of it as an underwater highway for sound waves. In this layer, sonar can hear whale songs on the other side of the globe.

In other layers, sound travels super slowly, making sonar work poorly. Submarines can hide well in these layers without being detected. The depth and location of layers change throughout the oceans.

affect sonar. A sonar system that works well in one underwater environment may not work in another. This makes sonar tricky.

In a warfare situation, submarines using sonar can find themselves in many different ocean environments. Because these ocean environments cannot be changed or controlled, submarines must be able to change and control their sonar and adjust it to work in the right environment. Scientists working to improve sonar systems for the future face three main challenges.

Shallow Water Sonar

Sending out a sound wave in shallow water is a little like throwing a ping-pong ball into a bucket—the waves bounce all over the place very quickly and may not bounce back to the sonar source. On top of that, there are often tides and currents in shallow waters, messing up sound signals. These things combine, making the use of sonar in shallow waters tricky. More hydrophones pointed in precise directions could help solve this problem in the future.

Bumpy Bottom Sonar

Sonar relies on incoming sound waves to interpret information about the surrounding environment. Sometimes the seafloor can be very bumpy, meaning it can be shallow for many miles and suddenly drop off into deep water. In these areas, some of the sound bounces back (in shallow areas) and some keeps going and going (deep areas). This leads to inaccurate sonar readings. In the future, better knowledge of the seafloor could help solve this problem.

The U.S. Navy operates a number of ships that specialize in using sonar to make detailed maps of the ocean floor. Above is a graphic showing the underwater mapping capability of one of these ships, USNS *Bowditch*. The *Bowditch* and others of its class are known as oceanographic survey ships.

Deep Water Sonar

In deep water, the seafloor can be very far away from the sonar source. This means the sound waves travel very far before hitting anything and are very weak by the time they return to their source. This can make interpreting information from the sonar signal difficult. For active sonar systems, deep water is especially hard. Future sonar systems specialized for deep water may need ultrastrong sound waves to provide clear returned signals.

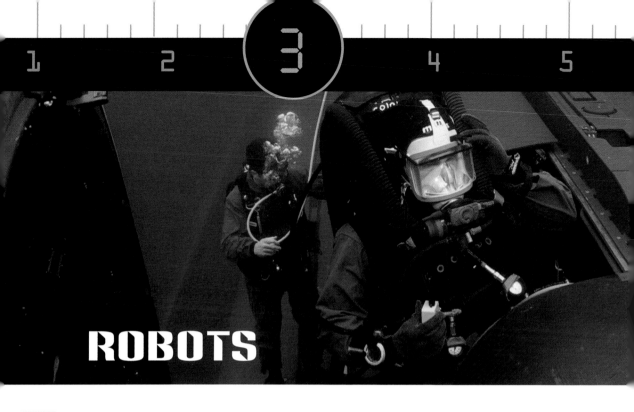

ROBOTS

Robots are powerful weapons for doing dangerous jobs in combat situations. Unlike human soldiers, they never hesitate to take risks and can be easily replaced. Today, the U.S. military uses robots in many different ways.

Modern robots aren't quite the machines we see in science-fiction movies. They're more like very smart machines that can move around by themselves. In the air, robotlike vehicles (including missiles with minds of their own) are very common. On the ground, crawling robots are programmed to hunt for minefields and dispose of dangerous bombs. Underwater, swimming robots search deep waters and explore the seafloor.

REMOTELY OPERATED VEHICLES

For many years, the navy has used underwater robots that are connected by a cable to the submarine or ship. These types of robots are called remotely operated vehicles (ROVs) because they have to be operated by remote control from a larger vessel.

Recently, the navy has ditched the remote control and created robots that operate by themselves. These robots are known as unmanned underwater vehicles (UUVs). Instead of operating on the end of a cable, UUVs are self-propelled, preprogrammed, and self-contained. You can give them a job and they will go off and do it. No questions asked. A few UUVs are in use today, and there are hundreds being developed for future warfare.

TODAY'S UUVs

Some UUVs look like torpedoes with fancy propellers. Others look like mechanical spiders that crawl on the ocean bottom. They come in many different shapes and can weigh up to 20,000 pounds (9,072 kg). Sensors, sonar devices, and cameras are mounted to modern UUVs so they can gather information.

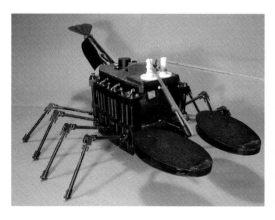

The RoboLobster is an experimental UUV that mimics the movement of a real lobster. In the future, the robotic crustacean might be used by the navy to crawl along the ocean floor in search of mines and other explosives.

The REMUS unmanned underwater vehicle was initially used by scientists to map the ocean floor, and then modified for military use. In March 2003, it teamed up with trained dolphins and human divers to clear the Umm Qasr port in Iraq of deadly mines. In the photograph above, an engineer assembles a REMUS.

UUVs do four main jobs for the military. First, UUVs survey an area and collect information about what sorts of ships or people are present. Second, UUVs help a ship or submarine navigate (and avoid hitting an underwater mountain, for example). Third, UUVs search areas underwater for dangerous mines. Finally, UUVs help track enemy submarines and other vessels in wartime situations.

One UUV that has already been put to the test is the remote environmental measurement units support (REMUS) UUV. The 80-pound (36 kg) REMUS UUV is specially designed to make maps of the ocean floor.

In 2003, in a harbor near Iraq, the U.S. Navy used REMUS UUVs to locate almost 100 man-made objects underwater. After the UUVs identified the objects, human divers checked if the objects were dangerous mines or harmless things such as rusty anchors and old truck tires.

This was one of the first times UUVs went to work during a war, but it is surely not the last. The REMUS UUVs helped identify bombs and keep the waters safe for ships and submarines. In the future, the navy plans to use UUVs to search for much more than just mines.

TOMORROW'S UUVs

There are hundreds of UUVs being developed by scientists and engineers today, each with a specific job in mind. Some UUVs are

COTS TECHNOLOGY

Until very recently, anything used on a U.S. submarine had to go through a long, strict screening process by the military. You couldn't just buy a computer and take it on board. You could only use computers that had been through the approval process—which could take years or even decades to complete. Over time, this meant many submarines were using old, out-of-date technologies.

Today, the military has approved the use of commercial off-the-shelf (COTS) technology. This change in policy saves the navy time (it doesn't have to wait for official approvals) and money (it's cheaper to buy a computer than develop and build it yourself), and helps to assure that the future submarines will have up-to-date technology.

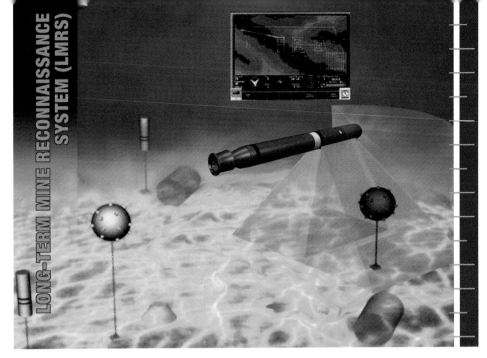

The Long-Term Mine Reconnaissance System (LMRS) is currently being developed by the navy. Since the LMRS is about the same size and shape as an MK48 ADCAP torpedo, it can be launched from an attack submarine's torpedo tubes. Its job will be to search the ocean floor for mines.

being designed as research tools to help us learn about the oceans. Others will be part of the navy's stash of underwater weapons.

UUVs have three separate parts: the vehicle, the sensors, and the steering. The vehicle is the main part of the UUV. Other parts of the UUV are connected to the vehicle. The sensors are the devices that collect different types of information. The steering is the navigation, guidance, and control pieces. It allows the UUV to operate without remote controls or tethers.

By tweaking the different parts of the UUV, scientists are creating new robots to do specific jobs. In the future, much work will be done to improve the sensors and the vehicle itself.

UNDERWATER GLIDER

The vehicle of most modern UUVs is a torpedolike structure complete with propellers. The downside of propellers is that they make noise that can be detected by an enemy in a combat situation.

To get rid of the noisy propellers, future UUVs may take the form of an underwater glider, which could "fly" silently through the water. A handful of underwater gliders are in development today. Although the shapes vary, all gliders have moveable wings that let them fly quickly for thousands of miles underwater.

Underwater gliders move by changing their weight, or buoyancy, while in the water. Taking in water lets a glider sink. Letting water out lets it rise toward the surface. These up-and-down motions and the angle of the wings allow a glider to move underwater the same way an airplane flies through the air. And since there are no propellers, the gliders are very quiet.

GLIDER SHAPES

So far, there are two basic types of glider shapes: torpedoes with wings and underwater airplanes. Many torpedo-type gliders have already been tested and are for sale by private companies. One called the Spray is designed to study the oceans and can travel for six months on its own. Another called the Slocum uses temperature changes in ocean water to create

The Slocum glider is seen from below in this underwater photograph. The Slocum is an example of a torpedo-type glider. It can swim just below the surface or dive down to a maximum depth of 6,500 feet (2,000 m). It is named after Joshua Slocum, who in 1898 became the first person to sail solo around the globe.

enough energy to fly for up to five years. Another, the Seaglider, is small enough to deploy from a small boat.

Underwater gliders shaped like airplanes are less common, but a few have been designed and tested. These shapes could be more durable when exploring unknown underwater areas. What will work best as a weapon for the navy? It seems they are still trying to decide in tests of their own.

In the spring of 2004, the Office of Naval Research (the science and engineering division of the U.S. Navy) tested some of its first gliders off the shores of San Diego, California. The navy says propellerless gliders could be used in the future to monitor long coastlines and search for mines in shallow waters during wartime.

SENSORS

The sensors on a UUV can be designed to look for almost anything. We already have UUVs that can search the seafloor for mines. The navy has also recently funded a project to create UUVs that can detect dangerous chemicals or microorganisms in the water. The idea is to use such a UUV as a defensive

ROBOT SCIENCE

Interested in creating your own underwater vehicles someday? There are many ways to do it, but one way is by becoming an ocean engineer.

Dr. Wayne Sternberger studied the oceans in college, then went on to apply his knowledge as a problem-solving ocean engineer. In his job he starts with a question about the oceans—such as how much chemical pollution is in seawater—and figures out how to answer it. In recent years he worked with a team of people to create and test UUV-based monitoring systems for the oceans.

Dr. Sternberger is also a student mentor with the Marine Technology Society (MTS). This organization shares information and educates people about technology in the oceans. To learn more about the MTS, go to http://www.mtsociety.org.

weapon. The UUV will gather information about what types of chemical or biological weapons an enemy has and what has already been released in a combat situation.

To create a chemical-sensing UUV, a team of scientists and engineers worked on the three basic parts of the UUV. First, the team created a sensor to detect tiny amounts of certain chemicals and biological agents in the water and tested it in a laboratory. Second, it came up with a way to mount the sensor on the vehicle. Third, it designed a device that could operate the UUV without a human at the controls. Then it tested the complete UUV to make sure it would work underwater for long periods of time.

If the navy likes how the test UUV works, a version of it could be used in future wars. The navy might also develop other UUVs to look for different types of chemical and biological agents. There are many different agents that could require many different UUVs.

Some engineers suggest that these technologies could be used in non-warfare situations, too. Instead of looking for a chemical weapon in seawater, a UUV could look for high levels of chemical pollution in the oceans. This could help us monitor the health of ocean water and keep it cleaner in the future.

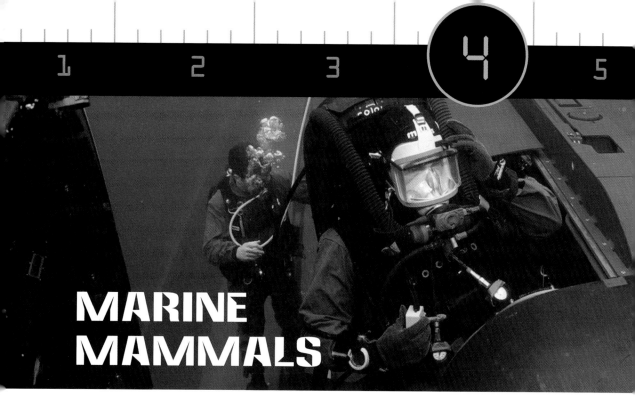

MARINE MAMMALS

In March 2003, the U.S. Navy faced a not-so-unusual wartime situation. It had to get a ship carrying food and supplies through a harbor possibly booby-trapped with mines. It was the beginning of the Iraq war and the residents of Umm Qasr were waiting for help. The U.S. Navy decided to deploy its fleet of mine-hunting dolphins to search the Umm Qasr harbor for bombs. Though the navy had been training dolphins to locate mines for decades, this was the first time the dolphins were used in a real combat situation. Working with divers and unmanned underwater vehicles, the dolphins helped clear the harbor of mines so the supply ship could safely pass.

NAVY MARINE MAMMAL PROGRAM

The Navy Marine Mammal Program (NMMP) began in 1960. The stars of the program are the bottlenose dolphins.

A bottlenose dolphin named K-Dog leaps out of the water in front of its trainer on March 18, 2003. K-Dog's unit was stationed in the Arabian Gulf as part of Operation Iraqi Freedom. The unit's objective was to clear the area of mines so that ships could arrive with relief supplies for Iraqi civilians. Attached to K-Dog's fin is an electronic device that allows the dolphin to be tracked while it swims underwater.

These animals are natural underwater athletes. They can swim up to 25 miles per hour (40 km/h) and dive 1,000 feet (305 m) deep.

Dolphins also have their own sonar system known as echolocation. They make clicks and whistles that travel through the water and bounce back, providing the dolphin with information about the surrounding environment. This system allows a dolphin to communicate, find its way, and identify objects in the water. The navy dolphins are specially trained to use their underwater talents to assist humans in wartime situations.

The future of the NMMP is a big unknown. Military research is under way to build robots that could someday replace the dolphins. So far, the machines aren't as smart as the dolphins, but as technology improves, the dolphins will be used less and less for military purposes. It seems unlikely, though, that machines will ever completely replace them.

TODAY'S MARINE MAMMAL SOLDIERS

Today's navy dolphins are trained to do many jobs, including finding enemy swimmers and locating and marking underwater mines. When tested, the navy says the dolphins are nearly perfect at marking mines.

Because mines come in all shapes and sizes, dolphins are not trained to look for one particular thing. Instead, dolphins are trained to look for, but not touch, any minelike object (something with metal and wires) and mark it. The markers are often small floats that are released and float to the surface where the

In addition to dolphins, the Navy Marine Mammal Program also trains sea lions. In this photo, a 375-pound (170 kg) California sea lion named Zak carries a device called a bite plate during a training session. The navy's sea lions help patrol harbors, looking out for enemy swimmers and any suspicious objects in the water.

dolphin's human teammates can see them. Once marked, navy divers are deployed to see if the object is a real mine.

More recently, navy dolphins have been trained to mark the location of mines with small radio devices. Specially trained divers called U.S. Navy SEALs (sea, air, land) can then map the locations of the mines on a computer. Later, divers attach remote-controlled explosives to the mines. They are blown up when all humans and dolphins are safely out of range.

TOMORROW'S MARINE MAMMAL SOLDIERS

Someday, the navy dolphins will be replaced by machines. This is for a number of reasons. In busy or cluttered waters,

GETTING INVOLVED

If you want to work with the Navy Marine Mammal Program (NMMP), you better start preparing now. The NMMP offers two unpaid training programs for college students that help them get started in the field.

The animal care and training intern helps NMMP staff prepare the animals' meals, maintain facilities, and sometimes assist in training the animals. The veterinary medical extern works with the navy's veterinary staff. This position requires that you complete a project in marine mammal medicine during your stay with the NMMP.

Both programs are very competitive. To learn more, visit the NMMP's Web site at http://www.spawar.navy.mil/sandiego/technology/mammals/interns.html.

A trainer demonstrates one of the many hand signals used to communicate with the navy's dolphins. Learning the various hand signals is one of the first steps in becoming a marine mammal trainer.

dolphins can get distracted from their jobs and take breaks to eat fish, follow passing boats, or play in the surf. On some occasions, large sharks or whales can scare dolphins, temporarily distracting them from their job. Machines, however, can't be distracted.

More important, the navy has decided it doesn't want its human divers or marine mammals in minefields where an accident could kill or injure them. Also, even though dolphins are much better than humans at working for long periods of time underwater, even dolphins get tired. A machine can continue working when the divers and dolphins have to rest.

DOLPHIN-BASED SONAR

The dolphin-based sonar (DBS) project is the navy's first step in building a machine to replace the dolphin. The DBS system attempts to mimic the dolphin's sonar system. The DBS sends out clicking noises similar to a dolphin's, and the sonar receivers (microphones that listen to the returning echoes) are spaced apart the same distance as a dolphin's ears.

When tested, scientists found that DBS can find objects on the seafloor and identify objects in the water about as well as a dolphin can. Computers help interpret the incoming signals and create rough images of objects in the water for humans to study.

Scientists found that the DBS makes less sound than most sonar systems. This is important because, unlike a real dolphin, a DBS cannot blend into the underwater environment. If the enemy were to detect the DBS, they would know the navy was near.

A bottlenose dolphin rests on a transfer mat before going out on a mission on March 17, 2003. The dolphin, named Spetz, was part of a team responsible for detecting mines in the Arabian Gulf. In the future, the navy hopes to use unmanned underwater vehicles to do the work currently done by dolphins.

BUILDING A ROBOTIC DOLPHIN

The navy says a robot that behaves like a dolphin is far in the future, but it is a goal for the U.S. military. To fully replace the dolphin, the navy needs a much smaller version of the DBS to gather information—one small enough to mount on a UUV. Plus, the UUV needs to be able to navigate on its own once deployed underwater. Only then will we be close to replacing a real dolphin.

By learning more about how dolphins work, the navy hopes to build better robots in the future. Understanding dolphin

The navy's Biosonar Project is the team behind the robotic dolphin. The robotic dolphin will consist of a dolphin-based sonar (DBS) system attached to an unmanned underwater vehicle. The robotic dolphin will not look like a real dolphin, but it will act like one.

sonar is still a big focus of research at the NMMP. In addition, scientists there continue to study how underwater sounds affect dolphins and other marine mammals such as whales, how to best care for dolphins in captivity, and how to breed the best dolphins for the job.

NONLETHAL WEAPONS

In March 2003, the U.S. military went to war in Iraq. Once the government of Iraq lost control of the country, many people began to steal and destroy public and private property. These actions contributed to the unsafe and chaotic state of the country. According to an international organization of experts called the Council on Foreign Relations, the U.S. military could have used more nonlethal weapons—weapons that stop people but don't kill them—to help keep peace in Iraq. If they are right, soldiers in future wars may use a lot more nonlethal weapons.

On land, nonlethal weapons are things like sprays that make people slip or stick to surfaces, rubber bullets that knock people out, and nets that trap and stop vehicles. These and many other nonlethal weapons have been used by the U.S. military with much success.

MAKING IT WORK UNDERWATER

Underwater, it's much harder to make nonlethal weapons work—you can't easily spray sticky goo underwater, for example—but it is possible. The U.S. military says no one is currently developing nonlethal weapons for use in underwater warfare. However, scientists believe that there is a promising nonlethal weapon that could work underwater in the future: sound.

By taking a close look at modern nonlethal land weapons that use sound, we can take a guess as to what types of nonlethal sound weapons could be used in the underwater wars of the future.

TODAY'S NONLETHAL SOUND WEAPONS

Sound travels in waves similar to the waves of the ocean, but sound waves are invisible to humans. Just as the size and shape of a wave of water can change (sometimes the surf is good, sometimes it's bad), the size and shape of a sound wave can also change.

Scientists often talk about the amplitude and frequency of sound waves. Amplitude means size. A large wave has a large amplitude, and a small wave has a small amplitude. The frequency of a wave is how close together the waves are. Short, closely spaced waves have a high frequency (waves occur more often) and long waves spaced far apart have a low frequency (waves occur less often).

Members of the U.S. Coast Guard participate in nonlethal weapons training exercises at Camp Lejeune in North Carolina. During the training, they practiced using guns that fire rubber bullets and grenade launchers that fire rubber pellets called sting balls. In the future, the military plans to increase its use of these and other nonlethal weapons.

As you change the size and shape of a sound wave, it takes on different qualities, some harmful to humans. Sound waves with very high or very low frequency cannot be heard by the human ear but can do funny things to the human body. Using these sound waves, the military has created sound-based, nonlethal weapons for use in land wars. There are four main types of these weapons in use today.

Infrasound

This type of sound is extremely low frequency. A low-frequency sound wave is so deep and so low that we cannot hear it, but it

THE JOINT NON-LETHAL WEAPONS PROGRAM

In 1997, the U.S. military created the Joint Non-Lethal Weapons Program. This program was designed to help the different branches of the military communicate what they know about nonlethal weapons. Today, the army, navy, marines, and coast guard cooperate in the program to share nonlethal weapons technologies and fund scientific research to create new weapons.

Much of the funding for research goes to scientists at the Institute for Non-Lethal Defense Technologies at Pennsylvania State University. Here, scientists design and develop new nonlethal weapons. They also test new weapons using computer models and help the military train soldiers to use them.

can make humans feel nauseated and confused. In the worst cases, low-frequency sound can damage internal organs and cause death. Plus, it is powerful enough to travel long distances through most buildings and vehicles, so there is no escaping it.

Acoustic Bullets

In this case, the "bullets" are actually low-frequency sound waves. All sound waves travel close to 700 miles per hour (1,127 km/h) in air. When shot in distinct bursts as a weapon, low-frequency sound waves can cause nausea and confusion. Unlike infrasound, acoustic bullets can be directed to specific areas.

Squawk Box

This weapon emits two separate, extremely high-frequency (ultrasonic) sounds that, when combined in the human ear, can cause nausea or fainting. What makes it especially useful is that it can be directed at a specific person within a crowd instead of blasting an entire group of people.

Curdler Unit

This is a device that produces a shrill, shrieking noise when plugged into speakers. Although it isn't quite loud enough to damage the human ear, it is enough to irritate and distract people. The military uses it to break up riots and enemy gatherings.

FUTURE NONLETHAL SOUND WEAPONS

The beauty of the sound wave is that it can travel through air, land, and water. Already, those planning the future of underwater warfare have outlined two potential uses of sound weapons at sea: to stop enemy swimmers and to stop enemy ships.

Using Sound to Stop Enemy Swimmers

Some nonlethal sound weapons used on land today, including infrasound, acoustic bullets, and the squawk box, could be tweaked for use on enemy swimmers.

The low-frequency infrasound and acoustic bullets can easily travel hundreds of miles underwater. Scientists are currently studying how such low-frequency sound waves affect the behavior of animals underwater. Whales have been studied the most, and scientists think sound can confuse and disorient whales underwater, causing them to get lost and beach themselves. In the future, if we can better understand the effect of sound on marine mammals, perhaps we could better use sound to confuse and disorient enemy human swimmers.

The current problem with infrasound underwater is that you can't direct it very well. Instead of hitting an individual person with a blast of sound, you would just flood the entire ocean with noise, possibly harming wildlife. Acoustic bullets could be directed better, but it's not clear how well this would work underwater.

The high-frequency squawk box might be a better option. The high-frequency waves can't travel as far through the water and could be directed to a smaller area. If it worked, this could go a long way in protecting wildlife from the harmful sound but still work to make enemy swimmers nauseous or faint.

Using Sound to Stop Enemy Ships

The U.S. Navy says that being able to stop enemy ships and submarines and establish safe zones in the water is the most important use of nonlethal weapons in future underwater warfare. A modified curdler unit kept on ships at sea might be a good choice for this type of job.

If some sort of curdler unit could be used from the surface of the sea to create a bubble of irritating sound around a ship, it might act as a barrier. Soldiers on board the ship would be exposed to the sound, but could be equipped with ear protection. Then anyone entering the bubble, including an enemy submarine full of sailors, would be forced to stop unless they had proper ear protection.

At this point in time, no one is testing these ideas because they are expensive and loud sounds can affect ocean life in ways we don't entirely understand. Plus, the navy says it is unclear whether nonlethal sound weapons or nonlethal barrier systems (such as giant nets used to stop enemy ships) will be the navy's best bet as a future nonlethal weapon. We will have to wait and see.

A scientist at the Center for Whale Research approaches a dead whale on a beach in the Bahamas. Scientists are investigating if navy submarine sonar is responsible for the deaths of numerous whales in the Bahamas and elsewhere. A major concern of using nonlethal sound weapons underwater is that the sound waves created by the weapon might unintentionally kill marine animals.

ASSESSING THE ENVIRONMENTAL IMPACT

The biggest problem with nonlethal sound weapons both on land and underwater is keeping the sound waves under control. When harmful sounds are projected long distances to stop oncoming crowds or ships, for example, all life in the area could feel the harmful effects. On land, this means friendly troops and civilians are sometimes affected. Underwater, this means marine mammals and other sea life could be in danger.

Learning exactly how sound affects marine mammals and other animals underwater is a hot topic in science research today. We know low-frequency sounds can travel across the entire ocean, making the world underwater much louder than we might think. We also know marine mammals and other animals often use sound to migrate, communicate, find food, and care for their young. Scientists wonder if too much underwater sound could endanger the ability of animals to function underwater.

In the past, when low-frequency sound systems (like navy sonar) were used near marine mammals in the wild, scientists discovered large numbers of beached whales on nearby shores. These events created lots of headlines in newspapers that navy sonar was killing whales. But whether low-frequency sound actually causes whales to get lost underwater and beach them-selves is still unclear. Until we know more about how sound affects life underwater, such sound-based weapons probably won't be widely used.

In 2002, the Natural Resources Defense Council (NRDC), filed a lawsuit against the U.S. Navy, hoping to stop it from testing a new high-frequency sonar system. The NRDC took action because it feared that navy sonar was harming marine life. The controversy over the navy's use of sound waves underwater is one reason that it is unlikely the navy will develop nonlethal sound weapons anytime soon.

THE FUTURE OF THE OCEANS

With all the thought and money going into underwater warfare research, it seems clear that submarines and the weapons systems they carry will be with us well into the future. And as these technologies improve and multiply, it's not crazy to think there will be more and more ocean-based wars in the future as well.

The more we learn about the oceans, the more we understand their value, and the more we realize how much we still have to learn. More than 70 percent of Earth is covered with water. That water is the largest habitat for life on the planet.

The ocean is home to single-celled critters called microbes as well as whales the size of train cars. We've only begun to understand our impact on it.

Because the oceans are largely unexplored and are home to so many different types of life, it's hard to monitor their condition. If we're not careful, we could destroy a new life-form before it is even discovered. In recent years, the military has become more and more aware of the value of the oceans.

As a result, part of developing new underwater weapons for future wars is testing how those weapons affect ocean life. Many scientists and military researchers are already testing how existing technologies impact animals like whales and dolphins.

In the future, the information scientists gather could be used to make more ocean-friendly weapons. That way, we can be sure underwater weapons are only harmful to the intended target, and not to our oceans.

GLOSSARY

active sonar A type of sonar that sends bursts of sound to detect objects underwater.

amplitude Refers to the size of a sound wave. Large waves have large amplitudes; small waves have small amplitudes.

antitorpedo A torpedo that destroys other torpedoes.

array An ordered group.

deploy To prepare and send out an instrument or weapon.

echolocation The use of high-pitched sound by dolphins and other animals to locate objects.

frequency Refers to how far apart sound waves are spaced. Short, closely spaced waves have a high frequency, and long waves spaced far apart have a low frequency.

hydrophone An underwater microphone.

nonlethal weapon A weapon that stops people or vehicles but does not kill them.

passive sonar Type of sonar that listens but doesn't make noise.

Remotely operated vehicle (ROV) A tethered robot often used by the military to search and collect information.

sonar A system using sound waves to detect and locate objects underwater.

stealth The act of being ultraquiet and moving without being detected.

supercavitation The process of vaporizing the water in front of a torpedo to increase its speed.

tether A cable connecting two things.

torpedo A bomb in the shape of an oversized bullet, with a propeller on one end.

ultrasonic A high-frequency sound wave that cannot be heard by the human ear.

underwater mine An explosive device that sits underwater until it is detonated by the sound or contact of a passing object.

unmanned underwater vehicle (UUV) The U.S. Navy uses this term to refer to self-propelled, preprogrammed, and self-contained robots.

FOR MORE INFORMATION

Association for Unmanned Vehicle Systems International
2700 South Quincy Street
Suite 400
Arlington, VA 22206
(703) 845-9671
Web site: http://www.auvsi.org

Navy Marine Mammal Program
Space and Naval Warfare Systems Center
53560 Hull Street
San Diego, CA 92152
(619) 553-2717
Web site: http://www.spawar. navy.mil/sandiego/technology/mammals

Office of Naval Research
One Liberty Center
875 North Randolph Street, Suite 1425
Arlington, VA 22203
(703) 696-5031
Web site: http://www.onr.navy.mil

Penn State University
Applied Research Laboratory
Torpedo Defense Programs Office
P.O. Box 30
State College, PA 16804-0030
(814) 863-3019
Web site: http://www.arl.psu.edu/capabilities/td.html

Submarine Force Liberty Museum
Box 571
Groton, CT 06349
(860) 694-3290
Web site: http://www.submarinemuseum.org

Submarine Warfare Division
2000 Navy Pentagon
Washington, DC 20350-2000
(866) 512-1800
Web site: http://www.chinfo.navy.mil/navpalib/cno/n87/html

Web Sites

Due to the changing nature of Internet links, the Rosen Publishing Group, Inc., has developed an online list of Web sites related to the subject of this book. This site is updated regularly. Please use this link to access the list:

http://www.rosenlinks.com/lfw/unwf

FOR FURTHER READING

Genat, Robert, and Robin Genat. *Modern U.S. Navy Submarines.* Osceola, WI: Motorbooks International, 1997.

Hossell, Karen Price. *Sonar.* Chicago, IL: Heinemann Library, 2002.

Mallard, Neil. *Submarine.* New York, NY: DK, 2003.

Payment, Simone. *Navy Seals: Special Operations for the U.S. Navy.* New York, NY: Rosen Publishing Group, 2003.

Presnall, Judith Janda. *Animals with Jobs: Navy Dolphins.* San Diego, CA: KidHaven Press, 2002.

Pringle, Laurence. *Chemical and Biological Warfare: The Cruelest Weapons.* Berkeley Heights, NJ: Enslow Publishers, 2000.

Wingate, Brian. *Submariners: Life in Submarines.* New York, NY: Rosen Publishing Group, 2004.

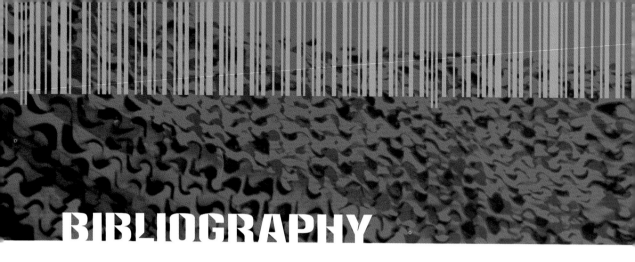

BIBLIOGRAPHY

Marcus, Jonathan. "U.S. Told to Boost Non-Lethal Arms." BBC News Online. February 26, 2004. Retrieved June 1, 2005 (http://news.bbc.co.uk/2/hi/middle_east/3489824.stm).

Meyers, Bernard, Frederick Cancilliere, and Kenneth LaPointe. "Torpedoes and the Next Generation of Undersea Weapons." *Undersea Warfare Magazine*, Winter/Spring 2002. Retrieved May 18, 2005 (http://www.chinfo.navy.mil/navpalib/cno/n87/usw/issue_14/torpedoes.html).

Naval Studies Board. *An Assessment of Non-lethal Weapons Science and Technology*. National Academy Press, 2003. Retrieved May 18, 2005 (http://books.nap.edu/catalog/10538.html).

Naval Studies Board. *An Assessment of Undersea Weapons Science and Technology*. National Academy Press. 2000. Retrieved May 18, 2005 (http://books.nap.edu/books/0309069262/html).

Naval Studies Board. *Technology for the United States Navy and Marine Corps, 2000–2035: Becoming a 21st-Century Force*. National Academy Press, 1997. Retrieved May 18, 2005 (http://www.nap. edu/html/tech_21st/uwindex.htm).

Office of Naval Research. "Future Naval Capabilities." 2004. Retrieved May 18, 2005 (http://www.onr.navy.mil/fncs).

Presnall, Judith Janda. *Animals with Jobs: Navy Dolphins*. San Diego, CA: KidHaven Press, 2002.

U.S. Navy Office of Information. *The Navy Unmanned Undersea Vehicle Master Plan*. November 9, 2004. Retrieved May 18, 2005 (http://www.chinfo.navy.mil/navpalib/technology/uuvmp.pdf).

U.S. Navy Office of Information. "Why We Need Submarines." Retrieved May 18, 2005 (http://www.chinfo.navy.mil/navpalib/ships/submarines/centennial/whysubs/whysubs.htm).

INDEX

W

About the Author

Krista West credits her lifelong love and interest in the sea to her father, a graduate of the United States Naval Academy and a career military officer. Today, she lives far from the ocean in Fairbanks, Alaska, and writes about marine biology, earth science, and ecology for kids and adults. Someday, she would love to take a ride on a submarine.

Photo Credits

Cover U.S. D.O.D graphic by Ron Stern, left corner and throughout © Digital Vision/Getty Images, top middle © Photodisc Red/Getty Images; p. 7 and throughout U.S. Navy photo by Chief Photographer's Mate Andrew McKaskle; p. 8 U.S. Navy photo by Photographer's Mate 1st Class Robert R. McRill; p. 10 U.S. Navy photo by Photographer's Mate 1st class David A. Levy; pp. 12–13 Commander Submarine Force U.S. Pacific Fleet/U.S. Navy; p. 15 © Bob Child/AP/Wide World Photos; p. 19 Photo courtesy Electric Boat/U.S. Navy; p. 20 Photo courtesy of Chris Oxley, Northrop Grumman Corporation/U.S. Navy; p. 24 U.S. Navy photo by Photographer's Mate 2nd Class Eric Lippmann; p. 27 U.S. Navy Graphic Illustration; p. 29 Office of Naval Research; p. 30 © Lisa Poole/AP/Wide World Photos; p. 32 © Boeing; p. 34 courtesy Webb Research/Office of Naval Research; pp. 38, 43 U.S. Navy photo by Photographer's Mate 1st Class Brien Aho; p. 40 U.S. Navy Photograph by Photographer's Mate 2nd Class Bob Houlihan; p. 41 U.S. Navy photo by Journalist 2nd Class Jessica B. Davis; p. 44 U.S. Navy Marine Mammal Program; p. 47 Coast Guard Petty Officer 3rd Class Zachary A. Crawford/U.S. Marines; p. 51 © Diane Claridge/AP/Wide World Photos; p. 53 © Jakub Moser/AP/Wide World Photos.

Designer: Evelyn Horovicz; Editor: Brian Belval